Escape the System

BY SHO OKUMOTO

By the same author, you can purchase other books of his through Amazon through this link here:

https://www.amazon.com/author/shookumoto

-For my mother

-This book is a work of fiction. Names, characters, places, and incidents either are products of the author's imagination or are used fictitiously.

Description

The day when life has given us a beat to our heart, our spirit giving life to our bodies, for us to begin our life journey as we enter this world, all innocent, with a pure soul, not knowing we have entered a world built by a system, created by the evil mastermind leaders.

Rules are created by the leaders for the people to follow and obey, as people get brainwashed, becoming sheep, and having no choice but to follow the system.

Having no bravery to escape the system, the people are trapped in the system, living in a prison, having no hope, no opportunities to grow out of the system, and living a miserable life.

To break and escape from the system, you must step out of your comfort zone, become the black sheep, and become a risk taker to be able to create your system in the world you live in, a system you truly believe in and to create your own rules and to ultimately become a self-made person.

One man, from the ghetto, from a broken family, surrounded by crime, who disagrees with the system and the rules, is on a mission, on an important journey, aiming to get out of the system, as he jumps on a wild rollercoaster ride, on the road to conquering greatness in his life.

The Beginning

The new world, as we enter the world of the unknown, a new life, a new beginning, as we scream in a high-pitched cry, born into this place called earth, producing our first ever communication cry using our newly made voice box, filling the white room with an annoying echoing sound, overworking everybody's eardrums who are present in the white room.

This is a world built by a system, created by greedy, corrupted, mastermind leaders, rules made for the people to obey and if they do not obey the rules, they will get punished. A rat race where people live in pain and exhaustion, trying to make a living, following their evil leader, listening to the leader's command, becoming fatigued as people carry out the task given to them and while doing their job, they will complain about their shitty leader tirelessly behind their back. But at the end of the day, they will still obey the rules like sheep, and the leader treats everyone like puppets.

Our wonderful loving parents teach us the basic lessons of the world we all live in. Our parents have also been brainwashed by the system, thinking the system is the only way to live life, built by rules, a prison where everyone is forced to enter sadly, unable to escape from the cold, dark prison, having no freedom.

Generation, after generation, passes down the rules of the system, and this basic knowledge about the dark system, the dark world becomes the normal teachings to the new child. People will reach a stage in their life, where they will not know what is right and what is wrong. People will not be able to think freely, not think for themselves, getting spoon-fed by the mastermind leaders and the only thing to believe in this corrupted world is the system.

Schools are the real beginning where the true meat of the system starts to get taught to the pupils, rules taught repeatedly, engraved in the pupils' brains, and the pupils knowing nothing, slowly get brainwashed into believing the system and start to follow the rules like sheep.

Pupils with high grades have a bigger chance of succeeding in life, maybe a chance of becoming a leader in a profession they have chosen, and having the power to create their system and create new rules for the people to obey and follow. The ones who are just average Joe or has low grades or have failed in their grades, all become soldiers, a slave to the system.

Rich people, in a relationship or having a family, are

all built by lies, having money, keeping everything together by the power of money and wealth and the poor people are in constant arguments, having no money to keep anything together, slowly becoming a broken relationship or a broken family.

I entered this world, innocent, just like all of you, with no knowledge of this world, like a brand spanking new computer, ready to get fed with rules from the system we live in, created by the leader.

My parents were poor, and we lived in the ghetto. Before I entered this world, my father was a small-time thug, doing petty crimes, trying to earn some dough and with enough dough earned, he would go to the brothel to enjoy some pleasurable entertainment. He met a woman who he truly liked and whenever he had enough dough, he will go back to the same brothel, and ask for the same woman, to have pleasurable fun. My father who is as thick as a brick, using no intelligence and only thinking with his sausage, wore no protection one day and pumped his love juice into the woman he liked, and got her pregnant. And that woman, when she was ready to give birth, she pushed out her very first newborn and that is when I entered this world crying and screaming in gibberish.

The privileged kids have the luxury to go to a beautiful, colorful park, filled with majestic trees, running around safely on a soft, spongy fresh green grass, filled with the pleasantly sweet aroma of freshly cut grass. Living in the ghetto, we don't have that type of privilege. I would play with my friends on the street, dodging sharp objects and broken liquor bottles, while we play prison-style rugby games. Another thing the privileged kids have the luxury of having is an awesome playground with a cool obstacle course. Living in the ghetto, you got to be very creative. We used to play at burned-down houses, creating games or playing hide and seek, and if there is a burned car on the street, we will pretend we are street racers and pretend we are racing down a quarter-mile drag strip.

My parents were bad and never truly took care of me, so I started to take care of myself and became independent at a tender age. I spent a lot of time on the streets with my friends and I quickly learned the system of the streets, learned to survive, becoming street-smart. We used to pickpocket people and with the cash we have stolen, we would go to the convenience store to buy some sweets and fizzy drinks. We all stopped going to school because we thought it was stupid and the streets became our true education. The fittest will survive on the streets and the weak will all become drug addicts or die on the street. I had basic reading and writing, nothing special, and not exactly a noble prize level of intelligence but enough to get around in this world comfortably.

Our house was always an empty, dark, cold, and lonely place to be. I truly hated going back home because it didn't feel like home. And if my parents were at home, it was just total mayhem. It is like visiting the safari and watching a male lion defending its territory. Our home is such a depressing and aggressive environment to be in. The constant arguments between my mother and father were terrible and never-ending. When my father drinks the devil's poison, he gets very violent, and aggressive and starts physically beating my mother.

One awful night, my mother and father roared at each other, arguments deafening the gunshots that were getting fired outside on the streets by the violent hooligans. They were both in the kitchen and my mother grabbed a cast iron skillet pan and smacks my father across the side of his head, knocking my father out cold, making him fall to the ground heavily, thumping onto the kitchen floor, lying unconscious and blood oozing out slowly from the side of his injured head. After the brutal incident, my ruthless mother invites her friends over to our house, leaving my father on the kitchen floor, as he bleeds, and making a puddle of blood around his head. My mother and her gang of friends start snorting the white snow, getting high, getting amped up, drinking like a fish, partying like there is no tomorrow, blasting sixties music, as everyone starts singing to the song getting played on the boombox, singing loudly in gibberish, everyone out of tune and having no rhythm.

Many times, I wanted to run away, escape from this miserable life, and fly to a magical place, a fantasy world, built by my dreams and to live a life I want to live and live in peace and happiness.

I would escape from my broken family and run to the library. I love the quietness, the peacefulness, surrounded by the magical books, and the aroma filling the library with a sweet, musky, and a hint of vanilla smell from the old books. Nice librarian smile filled with warmth and happiness. Every book is filled with a unique story, where stories become my way to escape from this sad world, giving me a new world, being discovered through the power of books and words giving me a dream, a fantasy where I can visit freely and stay in the dreamworld as long as I want to.

One of my favorite sections in the library, when I am not reading a book is the comic section. I would read endless comics, and the library is a wonderful place to choose something to read, sit, read, and stay for hours in peace away from hell.

The years rolled by, accepting my way of life on this planet earth, I have finally entered my wonderful teen years, perfecting the art of being the perfect teen, thought I had balls of steel, thinking I was bulletproof, big ego, and felt invincible. And around this time in my life, my father has become an entrepreneur. He has become a pimp. My mother stopped working at the brothel and worked for my father, working on the street as a prostitute.

One day, I was about to leave home, to go to my secret place, the library first before meeting up with my friends and my father orders me to work on the street. My father had one less woman working in his business because she caught an awful bad flu and my father needed to make money to reach his daily target. We argued and it was an argument I had no chance of winning. Sadly, I agreed, and my father took me to one of the houses he owns, where all the women who worked for my father lived together in a small house. One of the women who was starting work soon, I got paired up with her, who I will be working with, doing the same shift, she will be watching out for me, and guiding me in this sex trade. The woman dressed me up into a woman, and added makeup on me, making me look like a woman. When the woman and I were all ready to go, we left the house, walked to the woman's area on the street where it has become her territory, and I felt like a rugby player trying to walk in high heels. When we finally arrived at her special good-luck spot, we began our shift together.

This was a total nightmare. There was so much anger building up inside of me, boiling with rage and I can feel a fire getting lit inside of my heart. Here I am standing next to this woman, a prostitute, who is my guardian angel for today, a total stranger to me, and we are both going to engage in sexual activity with some low-life creepy men and for the services we have provided, we will get paid, and we will fill my stupid, greedy father's pocket with cash. And I bet my father will not pay me and he will pay the woman peanuts. At this point, I am raging with anger, and I could tear a man's head right off with my bare hands.

Cars drove past us, and I was praying and hoping no one will stop and choose me. Finish this miserable shift and I will run away from home and never return.

The woman was trying to work her magic, waving at oncoming cars, and whistling to potential customers but no luck. I got to admit, she was not attractive. All she was doing was chasing away potential customers and scaring them off. Which is good for me. The best way to describe my guardian angel is, she is a true junky, who needs to earn a bit of dough to feed her addiction.

After about an hour of standing around in this heat, sweat dripping off my chest, getting soaked into the fabric of my dress, creating a large sweat stain and it seemed like an eternity, suddenly a black Mercedes Benz pulls up, all tinted windows, couldn't see the inside of the car, and parks right in front of me. The woman pushed me from behind, making me move forward, as I slowly approached the rear door of the car. The rear door opened, and I hopped into the car. I didn't look around inside the car, and I sat in the backseat quietly and speechless. I smelt a strong odor of cigarettes, the smell of whiskey, and an old man's sweaty smell. I kept my head down, feeling so miserable, and depressed and my mind was empty, not knowing what to do. The car started to move forward, as the driver drove the car, which was a short trip and I sensed we haven't gone too far from the spot I got picked up from. The driver drove down a quiet discreet street away from the busy street, which is filled with nosy people.

I looked to my side, to see who this stinky man was, and I was sitting next to a bald man. The bald man was wearing a black suit, wearing round small glasses, had yellow rotting teeth, and had four grey hairs on one side of his bald head, combed over the top of his head, hoping to hide his shiny greased bald head. The old man looked at me, drooling, a creepy old bastard, who must have these crazy sexual desires and fetishes, swirling around in his filthy old mind of his, made a move and moved closer to me. The old man got into my personal space, breathing down my neck heavily, his breath was hot, which stunk like a long drop toilet and his hand immediately went downstairs and grabbed a hand full of my man goods.

The old man leaped back instantly, with a big surprise on his face, smiled creepily, and leaped forward toward me. The old man aggressively started to hug me, kiss me, and groped me. I am a teen boy and this old piece of garbage looked like he was in his seventies, a dirty prick, freaking hentai and if he has these disgusting sexual imagination desires to do this to me, I knew straight away he will not stop, who will become a dangerous predator, who will continue doing these sexual acts toward other innocent humans like me.

I needed to take action to become the hero to stop this madman, and I started to feel around my surroundings to find something to save myself from this madness as the old man continued to grope me. Lucky me, I found a gun in the old man's gun holster.

I quickly grabbed the pistol grip, pulled the gun out of the gun holster, brought the gun up, pressed the gun barrel into the old man's chest, pulled the hammer back, locked and loaded, and pulled the damn trigger happily. The loud bang, the gunshot fired at high speed, a new lethal bullet making an opening into the old flesh and entering the old man's old crusty chest, penetrating his flesh effortlessly, arriving and now bursting his disgusting, dirty heart, blood exploding out of his chest, flooding, and covering me in his warm awful red blood.

The driver looked back to see the action and I quickly pointed the gun toward the driver's head, pulled the hammer back, and pulled the trigger fearlessly, blowing the driver's head away, making his face unrecognizable and blood squirting out of his head like a water fountain, making a bloody mess inside the Mercedes Benz.

I pushed the old man off me, opened the rear door, hopped out of the car, and I went straight home. I was on a mission.

The sun was out, and the heat quickly dried the blood that covered me, I was still holding onto the gun, as people on the street watched me in shock. It is the ghetto, so witnessing a crime, is not a big deal. Many bad things happen around here and lots of criminal activity happens in this part of the city. But as the people looked closer at the figure, getting more curious, now getting a clear view, seeing a teen covered in blood, carrying a gun, and walking somewhere with a purpose is not what you see every day. This will send shock waves up the spines of the people witnessing this.

I arrived at my house finally, opened the unlocked front door and I entered my house. I heard lovemaking inside the house, and it was a terrible sound to come home to. I followed the sound, which led me to the lounge, and I saw my unfaithful father and the woman with who he was making love, she works for my father. The reason I know this is that I saw that woman earlier today at the house I visited before my shift started. My father and the woman were going at it like rabbits on the couch, using their stored-up love juices ready to be released today at any moment, and my father must have sensed there was someone else present in the lounge, looked up, and looked straight into my eyes. My father stopped pumping his red sausage into the woman's glory hole and I was disgusted at what I saw, raised my weapon hand, and pointed the gun barrel straight toward my father's head. I pulled the hammer back and at this point, a million things were going through my mind, and everything I was thinking about gathered into a small ball, and the ball of thoughts has become hate. I saw fear in my father's eyes for the first time in my life and I watched him move his mouth, trying to calm the storm. I have become God, and I have the power to delete a human being from this world. My vulnerable father talked repeatedly in a gentle, scared voice, and the more he talked, the more my anger kept rising. With so much rage, my anger silenced his nonsense, my mind was clear as a crystal blue ocean and I knew exactly what was right and what was wrong. Hate toward my father made me pull the trigger, firing a dangerous angry bullet toward my father's head and I watched the shiny bullet do its job, blowing my father's brainless head away, watching blood squirt up and blood showering everywhere in the lounge and the naked woman getting covered in my father's blood. The woman screamed in shock and fear, pushed the dead headless corpse off her, grabbed her clothes, and ran and exited out of the house butt naked. This is the beginning of the new me.

I moved out of my house, the same day I killed my father and I started to live on the streets, studying and learning more deeper into how the streets operate, becoming more street-smart. Word got around quickly on the street, and I made a name for myself, and a crew, an organization wanted me to join them. So, I did. Becoming a small-time gangster, learning the ropes, learning the game called hustling by the leaders of the crew. I was young, hungry, and wanted to hit the big time fast, to have the luxury that I always wanted, and to have money showering all over me endlessly through hard work.

Years went by, breaking the law, and cheating to earn money, I quickly climbed the ladder in our crew, and I got accepted, got introduced, and started to work in another section of the organization. It was the drug business. You got to be fearless and ruthless in this game and only the chosen few gets selected for this honor.

The crew I was part of had connections with the Asian mafia and the leaders of our crew had agreed to do the drug business with the Asian mafia. The plan is the Asian mafia will supply the drugs and sell them to our leaders. From there, our crew will distribute the drugs onto the street. If successful, there will be a copious amount of cash made.

Since I was the lowest-ranked member in the drug business, I had to fly to Siam to meet up with the Asian mafia, and collect the marijuana, which was given as a sample for our leaders to test out first before moving forward with the deal. Our leaders are not just buying small amounts, they are buying crates of drugs from the Asian mafia, so they must test it first, be happy with the product, and if satisfied, they will continue forward with the business deal. Both parties need to be satisfied. This is the seventies, so the customs at the airport are not strict and we have a very good chance of smuggling drugs from Siam into our home country. Play it smart, beat the system, and play the cards right and we should succeed.

On my first trip to Siam, my first meeting with the Asian mafia, I got the goods and I had to think of how to bring the goods into my home country without getting caught. I was back in my hotel room, thinking about how to hide the package filled with marijuana. I thought for a while and I found a perfect-sized radio in my hotel room, small enough to fit into my bag. I unscrewed the screws in the radio, took the radio apart, took all the radio parts out, just leaving two plastic casings and I put the package into one casing, which fit perfectly, and put the other casing on top, screwing the screws back into the radio. Now, we are game.

On the day of my flight back to my home country, leaving Siam was easy peasy Japanesey. Landing in my home country, arriving at the airport, hopping off the airplane, and going through customs, my hands started to sweat, and my heart was pounding so hard, it felt like it was about to burst out of my chest. I approached the customs officer, becoming more nervous, feeling my legs getting heavy and everything starting to slow down, feeling I was moving in slow motion, and finally what felt like a million years, I stopped and faced the customs officer.

The customs officer looked like a nice bloke, an easy-going, free-spirited person. It could be just an image thing, selling a lie, and could be one evil bastard. The customs officer asked a few questions, which were easy to answer, and with every answer I gave, I got a green light tick. Finally, when I thought we were finished and thought I was good to go, the customs officer wanted to check my bag.

Now, I thought to myself, I am screwed. I handed my bag to the customs officer, and he grabbed my bag, opened the bag, searched around inside the bag, while sniffing at the same time, and finally grabbed the radio out of my bag. The customs officer looked at the radio with curiosity, examining the radio thoroughly and what the customs officer was thinking in his mind, I will never know, and I thought to myself, I was going straight to jail. The leaders I was working for, would just laugh if I went straight to jail, because I am just a low-ranked member in this drug business, and I am replaceable. I am just a soldier, a slave serving my leaders. The customs officer finished examining the radio and I was thinking of the worst outcome, thinking of a terrible punishment that I will be receiving very soon. To my surprise, the customs officer puts the radio back into my bag, zipped my bag closed, gave my bag back to me, and he smiled at me, telling me I am free to go. I am now free and as I walked filled with happiness, I just pulled off a job successfully, I exited and left the airport, grabbed a taxi, and headed back to the gang headquarters, where my leaders are waiting for my arrival with the goods.

At the gang headquarters, I handed the goods to the leaders, and they took apart the radio, took the package out, opened the package, rolled up a fat joint, and smoked and tested the marijuana. The leaders discussed the quality of the marijuana, getting high and stoned, and finally, the leaders made their minds up. The leaders decided to move forward with the business deal.

In the final stage of the discussion between the Asian mafia and the leaders, they both agreed with the deal, both parties were extremely happy with the business deal, and big shipments are now going to arrive at our shores.

On the day of the shipment, the Asian mafia delivered the goods by their aircraft and dropped the goods from the aircraft into our territorial waters. The leaders had sent out just enough speed boats and people including me to pick the goods up and bring the goods back to the gang headquarters. This was all done during the night.

Back at the gang headquarters, we would unload the crates off the speed boat, and stack the crates neatly in the storeroom. Next stage, we will open the crates, take out the Buddha sticks, which are the delicious Siam marijuana wrapped around a thin bamboo stick, and have been tied together by a hemp string and dried slowly. We would cut the hemp string, pull the Siam marijuana apart carefully, weigh them to the correct weight for distribution, pack the weighed marijuana and we will sell this potent marijuana on the streets. Our crew made a killing.

Loads of cash were made and flowed into our little organization, putting big fat smiles on our leaders' faces. With such big success, the leaders thought it was the best time to expand their business and grow their organization. Greed takes over the leaders' minds, wanting to take all the pieces of the pie, make more money and ultimately have complete power over everything.

Since I was still a low-ranked worker in the drug business, I had to fly back to Siam to meet with the Asian mafia and bring cocaine back to my home country for my leaders to test out. At this point, I was not happy with my job, and I sensed how corrupt and heartless my leaders are. No matter how hard you work, working ridiculous hours, getting no appreciation from the leaders, no days off, because even on your days off, you are on call and you will get called up to work again doing some stupid work for the leaders, and you still get shitty pay, and for some reason, I am not moving up like I was before. It is as if the leaders don't want me to move up in the drug business.

I flew back to Siam and same as the first round, I met with the Asian mafia and got the cocaine samples for my leaders to test out. I was back at my hotel room, and I reflected, while drinking strong liquor on how I almost got caught bringing the marijuana into my home country. I am a hundred percent sure the customs officer knew I had packed the marijuana into the radio because the smell reeked and the marijuana is so potent, just smelling it will get you high as a kite and make you super stoned.

I remember the customs officer looking at me, looking at a young fella, who gave me a few nods, and I got a slap on my wrist, and he let me go. But if this time I walk through customs carrying cocaine and if I get the same customs officer, I will be very unlucky and I will be screwed because there is no second time lucky, and cocaine is a big no-no.

The sixties and the seventies are a time when there were lots of hippies who smoked copious amounts of marijuana, considering marijuana as pleasurable and benign. To be honest, everyone smoked marijuana.

I need to plan quickly and since I was not happy with the organization and I was unhappy working for my leaders, disliked the crew I was part of, and truly hated the leaders, I need to make two important plans. So, it is time for me to pick my balls up off the ground, step up my game and take over the crew and the organization. To be able to run my crew, to become the new leader, to make new rules for my soldiers for them to obey and follow, and to build a system in the organization that I believe in. I am tired of following my leaders and obeying their stupid rules which I don't want to follow, and I hate following a system I disagree on. Kill the leaders who own the organization, and I will become the new leader, creating a whole new organization.

That will be the second thing to do on my to-do list. Right now, the priority is to get the cocaine into my home country. So, I hired a beautiful Siam woman who is drop-dead gorgeous. I bought her a ticket back to my home country. We both made a deal, and we are in business.

On the day of our flight to my home country, the Siam woman was standing in my hotel room, wearing just a bra and her underwear, with heels laying on the floor next to her. I packed the cocaine into small clear zip-lock plastic bags and hid the plastic bags in her bra, underwear, and inside her heels, packing them neatly and evenly. I checked the result, looking at the Siam woman to make sure everything looked legit, and I watched the Siam woman, as she got dressed, putting her heels on and we are game. She looked exquisite, dressed naturally, and looked normal and legit.

We went to the airport, boarded the plane, leaving Siam and as usual, it was very easy. Landing in my home country and arriving at the airport, both of us hopped off the plane, we walked through customs, everything going smoothly, and my plan might just work.

Men and customs officers who were men, stared at the Siam woman, and their jaws dropped watching an elegant, beautiful woman, having the same beauty as a supermodel, walking past the men, men continuing to drool over the Siam woman and the only thing the men were thinking about, was something very dirty which only men could imagine about.

Like a gentle breeze, with no interference, we succeeded, exiting the airport, grabbing a taxi, and now, heading to the gang headquarters.

At the gang headquarters, in the leaders' office, the Siam woman was in the office shower, undressing, taking the packed cocaine out of her bra, underwear, and heels. The Siam woman quickly got dressed, grabbed the packed cocaine, opened the office shower door with one hand, with the other hand carrying the packed white snow, walked out of the office shower, and handed the packed cocaine to the leaders.

I couldn't hold back my anger toward the leaders and me being a hot-headed person, I spoke what I wanted to say, and I started to have a bit of a long discussion with my leaders. The conversation started to get louder, getting heated up by our anger, and the talking started to sound like three men barking at each other like wild dogs. The office felt like a pot of boiling water, ready to erupt and the top was ready to blow off at any time. Men are not intelligent enough to have a verbal discussion and end the conversation in agreement. We are wild animals, all brawn and no brain and the only way to settle this argument is through the art of scrapping each other out. The winner of the brutal fight will be victorious in the argument, making that person right and the brutally beaten loser wrong. The leaders had enough, and I was just pissed off. All three of us, staring at each other, eyes filled with flames of rage, we all lost our patience, and next, all hell broke loose.

All three of us ripped our guns out of the gun holster, two men pointing their guns at me and I pointed my gun at the leaders, going side to side, ready to shoot whoever made the first move. At a flick of a switch, hell erupted, and we started to shoot away, shooting at each other, like the real wild west, the real Mexican standoff, all in, shooting away like a bunch of mad men. Creating a blood bath, as the Siam woman witnessed a bloody massacre right in front of her, blood squirting everywhere around in the office, bits of flesh getting torn off our bodies by the hot slicing bullets that have just missed our major organs that are keeping us alive and standing. All three of us going autopilot shooting non-stop, the pain becoming numb and before all this craziness started, the Siam woman thought she was about to start a new life. The Siam woman was ready to start a new journey in her life, which I told her I will give to her when I hired her in Siam, and now, she might be regretting her decision. Most likely now, she wants to escape from this bloody massacre and jump on the first plane back to Siam.

All three of us, the dumb shooters, peppering each other with bullets like idiots with no good plan, adrenaline pumping through my veins, feeling the hot bullets penetrating my body, I saw a flash of green light straight in front of me, as one leader goes down as I shot a bullet straight into his throat and blood bursting out of his throat. Lucky me, lucky shot. I shot the next lucky bullet straight into the second leader's head and his head exploded a fountain of blood up toward the office ceiling. He dropped down, sinking deep down to the burning gates of hell, as he joins with his useless partner. I am the winner, the last man standing.

Feeling proud of myself, I looked over to the Siam woman, I smiled at her, and she managed to smile back at me, but behind her smile was fear and shock and I looked up at the office ceiling. A bright flash of white light flashed in front of my eyes, and I moved my eyes toward the light bulb in the ceiling. My muscles in my legs let go, lost all my strength in my legs, becoming jelly and I dropped and fell toward the office floor, crashing into the ocean of darkness, sinking deep down into the dark waters of the unknown, a place where fear is everywhere, where no human being can escape from the fear that surrounds them. The light started to close slowly until finally, darkness filled the room.

The Finale

The angry clouds move aggressively through the dark sky, thunderstorm forming as the warm, moist air rises into the cool air, and in a blink of an eye, thunderstorm erupts violently, causing thunderbolts to strike down into the dark world, a flash of lightning and the crash of thunder continuously destroying happiness and giving fear to the lost mind.

I was all alone, fear building up inside of me, a thunderstorm disappearing instantly as if someone has turned the tap off on the sink and I was surrounded by darkness, filled with freezing air, as I breathe out a small misty cloud out of my mouth. I walked around in total darkness, a place with no ends, no destination, only a dark space of the infinite universe, where there is a beginning and a never-ending journey. Not a single sound in this universe and the only thing I can hear is my voice in my head, talking to myself in confusion and I am the only human being walking around lost in the dark world. I walked around with fear, and confusion, trying to find something, trying to find some sort of life form or some light to see where the hell I was.

Suddenly an instant electric shock strikes my heart painfully. The electric shock and the pain, automatically pulled me down to my knees, crashing my knees down to the hard ground and I had no control of my body as pain took over my body. With the little energy I had in me, I was able to bring both my hands up to my chest, pressing my chest, feeling my rapid heart beating away like a thrash metal drummer, and I was in excruciating pain. Painful tears started to form and started to roll down both my cheeks and zap. Another sharp electric shock strikes me again straight into my vulnerable heart and the electric shock made me spread my arms out to the sides like a bald eagle ready to fly down and grab its meal. I tilted my head back, still in pain and I looked straight into the dark sky and bang.

A bright flash of light filled my eyes, and I got sucked straight back instantly, moving at the speed of light and snap. I woke up, gasping for air and the oxygen mask, pumping oxygen into my mouth, I was able to start breathing normally, regaining consciousness, and tasting the tasteless oxygen.

The loud ambulance siren screamed through the streets, racing to the hospital like a bullet train and I saw the paramedics working on me, trying to save my life. Time moved rapidly, at a pace where the mind is trying to gather the lost pieces, to put the puzzle back together, a body lying on the stretcher, useless and the only thing I was thinking about, as I lie on the stretcher was my next destination. The afterlife. I felt a soft, gentle, light as a feather hand, producing a neutral flow of energy, grab my hand, gently pulling me out of the real world and I felt my body becoming light, weightless, like an astronaut floating in space, slowly standing back up, exiting from reality and finally, I stood next to the paramedic, inside the speed demon ambulance. I looked down and saw myself, dying on the stretcher, bleeding to death, and looking like I was ready to go to the afterlife at any time.

How was this possible? Was I dead already? Am I dreaming? Is this a nightmare? I looked at the heart rate monitor unit screen and my heart was struggling to keep me alive, as it beat away, pumping blood around my body, trying to survive.

I stood in confusion, worried, inside the ambulance and I felt emotionally sad watching myself dying in the back of the ambulance. I heard a sound, a sound very familiar to my ears, a recognizable sound, and I looked straight back to the heart rate monitor unit screen, as it screamed telling the paramedics, my heart has stopped beating.

Immediately the paramedic next to me, grabs the defibrillator paddles, placing one paddle to my right sternum, just below my clavicle, and placed the other paddle just below my left nipple, along the anterior-axillary line and zap.

Back to the darkness, but only this time, I was comfortable in the world of my dreams, with no fear and the next thing I hear was a loud beeping sound started to sing away a melody I recognized, like a roaster crowing, a wake-up call and I slowly opened my eyes.

I was lying in my bed, looking up at the ceiling, feeling the new day, fresh crisp morning air filling the room, sunbeam entering my apartment room, filling my room with natural light with warmth and comfort. I smiled, felt relief, and smelt and tasted success. I looked around to make sure I wasn't dreaming and sure enough, I was back in reality, alive, a survivor of the bloody massacre. I got up, hopped off my bed and I exited my room, walking around my apartment room and everything looked normal and the same. I spotted a woman's bra on my black leather couch, and I recognized the bra, but I have forgotten who it belonged to. I was working my brain, flicking through my memory photo album, trying to find the owner of the bra. The light bulb in my mind did not light up and my brain is dazed. It is not important now, and I am sure the owner of the bra will turn up at some stage or she will contact me to collect the bra. I looked down to see what I was wearing, and I was wearing the same clothes that I wore on the day of the massacre. I guess, I got released from the hospital, came back to my apartment, and just comatose on my comfy bed until I had enough energy to wake up and start my new chapter in life.

I heard the front door to my apartment room getting unlocked and I headed to the front door to see who it might be. The front door opened, and the cleaner walked into my apartment room, putting her cleaning tools down near the entrance and leaving my apartment room, and leaving the front door open. She is my cleaner who cleans my apartment room, and she must be getting more cleaning tools. Everything looks normal to me, and I am back from hell, ready to step into the reality, the reality that I have unfinished business I needed to sort out. I exited my apartment room and headed to the bar on foot. The bar will be the best place to look into first, to get some solid answers.

The bar used to be owned by the leaders who I worked for in the past and since I killed them at the massacre, I technically own the bar, the crew, and the organization. Since I was absent for some time, I believe someone else has taken over and a new leader is running the bar, the crew, and the organization. They probably think I am dead as well.

I will show up at the bar, show my face, and take what is truly mine because I am the man who killed the leaders, and I am the new leader and I own everything now.

The sun has risen into the crystal-clear blue sky, heating the city morning, people sweating from the heat, tears of hate rolling down their cheeks, as everyone is commuting to a job they hate, living in a system, controlled by the leaders and people being sheep, the followers, a slave to the system and the leaders using the people like puppets.

I arrived at the bar and the bar is always open from eight in the morning for the alcoholics to jump on the bandwagon with the others of the same kind and hit the booze hard to see where the day takes them.

You are either part of the rat race or you are part of the underworld, and the bar is also where dirty businesses are discussed, and a place where criminal organizations, corrupt cops, and corrupted powerful people have their meetings.

I was about to open the entrance door to the bar when a young gangster pushes the entrance door open from the inside, exiting the bar and walking away from the bar. I walked straight into the bar before the entrance door closed shut.

The bar had a musky smell, mixed with tobacco, oak wood, and alcohol aroma lingering in the bar, with ambient lighting. One stocky tatted-up bartender working, and a few regulars inside the bar drinking.

Not busy, just a normal regular morning crowd of alcoholics.

I walked straight over to the bar counter, sat on a bar stool and I made eye contact with the bartender. I pointed at the beer I wanted to drink, off the beer tap, closed all my fingers, and raised my index finger, sending a message to the bartender, the number one signal, telling him I want one pint of beer. The bartender gave me the thumbs up.

I was relaxed, mind cool and empty of thoughts, daydreaming as I waited for my pint of beer, sitting on the bar stool happily and I felt an unwanted presence standing behind me, who stunk of cigarettes, breathing down my neck heavily. I kept my cool, trying to ignore the unwanted presence behind me, observing the bar, for now, to learn who is running this joint.

I watched the bartender open the bar fridge, grab an ice-cold pint glass, walk over to the beer tap, tilt the pint glass at a forty-five-degree angle, pour the fresh crisp beer into the center of the pint glass, leveling the pint glass once it has reached halfway and pours the beautiful beverage till the pint glass is filled nicely.

The bartender puts the freshly poured pint of beer down on the bar counter and pushed a pint of beer toward me. I watched the pint of beer gracefully slide across the smooth varnished walnut wood bar counter, the liquid refreshment not spilling a single drop and I watched the pint of beer slide past me. I was surprised and the elegancy of the pint of beer sliding past me distracted me from catching my pint of beer. Suddenly, in the corner of my eye, I saw a large hand, like a bear's hand, hairy and looked like a coal miner's hand and in the most perfect timing, the pint of beer, entered the coal miner's hand. The hand closed, gripped tightly, and lifted the pint of beer off the bar counter. I heard the man, who was standing behind me, chugging down the freaking beer that I ordered.

I stood up off the bar stool, anger fueling my heart, adrenaline pumping through my veins, and I clenched my fist tightly ready to knock the living daylights out of this rude bastard and send him off to the stars of hell. I turned around slowly like a second hand on a clock, ready to unleash hell, and now finally facing the man who stole my pint of beer, I looked at this man and I got a complete shock.

The man looked like a sasquatch, who looked like he just came out of his hiding place, returning to civilization.

Seeing this sasquatch standing in front of me, I had no chance of knocking this man out and if I tried, every bone in my precious hand will get destroyed and break into millions of pieces, making my hand useless for a fight I will have no chance of winning. Any strikes I throw at him, he will not feel a single thing. I need something hard and solid to destroy this sasquatch.

I looked down to my side and saw the bar stool I was sitting on before and as I was about to pick the bar stool up to swing as hard as I can at the sasquatch's head, hoping to knock the living daylights out of this sasquatch, I heard the entrance door to the bar busted open aggressively and immediately gunshots getting fired, firing away, peppering inside the bar.

Top shelf alcohol bottles getting smashed by the angry bullets and I quickly ducked for cover, and I witnessed the sasquatch, who was standing in front of me, getting peppered by the bullets, blood squirting out of his gunshot wounds and finally the big boy, slowly dropped down to the bar floor, crashing and sinking to the burning gates of hell.

I quickly turned around, looking straight toward the entrance of the bar, and saw two shooters, all dressed in black, and faces covered in a black balaclava, both holding a Tommy gun, old school, and the only crew that uses the Tommy guns were the crew I used to be part of. Perfect timing for me and this was my perfect chance to get the solid answers that I am looking for.

The two shooters looked around inside the bar, making sure they did their job properly like true professionals, and they didn't spot me, lucky me and they both looked satisfied and made a run for it. I quickly got up, bolted straight toward the entrance of the bar, dodging the destroyed tables and bar stools, exited the bar, and followed the two shooters.

I kept a good distance from the two shooters, making sure I don't get seen following them, and finally when I saw the two shooters arriving at their destination, I quickly hid, out of sight, spying on the two shooters and they have arrived at the gang headquarters, which used to be owned by the leaders I killed.

The two shooters took their black balaclavas off and I have never seen them before. Must be new blood. I watched the two shooters opening the door and entering the gang headquarters and I bolted straight toward the door, before it closes, just in case the door locked itself. I managed to reach the door before it closed, squeezed myself through between the closing door and the door frame, and now I entered the gang headquarters and the door clicked shut.

At this point, I didn't care about the two shooters. I wanted to know who was running this organization.

If there is a new leader, there will be another Mexican standoff, another shootout, another bloody massacre will erupt again and I will come out victorious, to take the throne to become the king of the jungle, the master, and everyone who works for me must obey my rules, follow my system and I will control my soldiers.

I sneaked around the gang headquarters, not getting caught and I finally arrived at the most important room, the leader's office. The office door was slightly opened, and I could hear lovemaking happening. I squeezed through the opening, entered the leader's office and I followed the sound, walking toward the couch.

Two people making love passionately on the couch, a man on top of the woman, and I quickly recognized his face. He is the most famous and the most powerful drug lord in this country. The man got swept, landing on the couch and a beautiful woman took the top position. My eyes were glued to the woman in shock and surprise. Not because of her natural beauty. It is because it was the Siam woman who I hired.

The Siam woman was distracting the man, with her natural beauty and the pleasurable actions she was giving to him, and less than a minute, the Siam woman reaches out to the side with her hand, grabbing a paper-knife off the small wooden side table which was located next to the couch. The man was resting his head on the top edge of the couch, enjoying the view, blinded by the joy of lovemaking and he had no idea what was going to happen next. The Siam woman went from moaning with pleasure, face quickly turned dark, evil, cold-hearted devil, gripping the paper-knife in a forward grip tightly by her side and in one motion, sliced the man's throat, blood instantly squirting out of the man's throat, covering the naked Siam woman in blood.

The Siam woman ruthless, stared at the man, the most famous and the most powerful drug lord in this country, as he was gurgling for breath, slowly dying, bleeding out his life, getting closer to death, and preparing himself to go to his next destination, the afterlife.

The Siam woman got off the dead man, dropped the bloodstained knife onto the office floor and she went over to the office desk. The Siam woman pressed a button on the office wireless intercom and spoke to a man, who is a soldier, a worker, telling him to chop the dead body up into nice small pieces and to feed it to the starving pigs. The man obeyed the command, the conversation ended and the Siam woman, who was naked, and covered in blood, walked over to the office shower, opened the door, entered the office shower, and closed the door shut. I waited for a minute, and when I heard the water showering down, that is when I took the opportunity to make a move.

I looked around the office quickly, before the men arrives to the office to collect the dead body and kept my ears wide open, to hear when the Siam woman has finished having a shower. I was looking for answers to what is going on and I must have missed a lot because what I have just witnessed is some crazy mayhem.

I went over to the office desk, and I was searching for answers, looking for something that will lead me to the big pie. Having no luck, I stood up straight, and behind the office desk, a meter to the right side away from the office desk, I saw a small wooden cabinet facing into the office. On top of the small wooden cabinet, had a magical display of a Butsudan, a Buddhist altar, beautifully handcrafted. Surrounding the Butsudan, was a candle in a candle holder, an incense stick placed in an incense holder, a Tibetan singing bowl, some fruits in a small bowl, and a cup of tea. It is a place for prayer to pay respect to someone close to you who has died.

I looked deeper into the Butsudan to see the face photo and I wanted to know who the Siam woman was praying to, and who she was paying respect to. The closer I got to the face photo, my eyes adjusting, now, getting clear visibility, my jaws dropped instantly. The face photo was me. My face photo was framed and the engraving on the wooden photo frame had my full name, the year I was born, and the year I died. The candlestick was lit, glowing in the office and the incense stick burning slowly, filling the office with the magical aroma of wildflowers.

I was stunned, speechless, and confused again but even more. Am I truly dead? But everything surrounding me, this whole time felt so real. I was trying to convince myself that I wasn't dreaming and if I was dreaming, this is one hell of a nightmare and I will be pissing my pants like a kid who has just watched the 1973 horror film, The Exorcist.

I thought for a second. All the looks by the people from the real world, were they not for me? Was it for the person who was behind me? Did I fit into this world of reality not knowing that I was a ghost?

I have heard when a person dies unexpectedly, and when the ghost remains in the real world, it has not found inner peace, because it has not accepted the truth and the truth was, they have died. They live in a dream surrounded by reality, writing and living in a world of fantasy, creating a lonely planet, where you cannot mingle with anybody. As loneliness starts to chew your soul, you are lost in an infinite life, filled with misery, time disappears becoming endless, a prison built by you and the only way to free yourself from the chains of sadness, locked onto your wrists and ankles, chained you down in the lonely prison, is to find your inner peace. To be able to walk and enter through the afterlife, the universe where others like you live in the stars of peace and harmony.

I closed my eyes, reflecting on the first time I met the Siam woman. She was working on the street, as a prostitute, working for a sleazy pimp and when I saw her standing on the street, I knew she was the one and I knew I have found my perfect woman.

I offered the Siam woman a new life I will be giving to her, giving her the freedom, to walk away from the system, to follow no rules, and to become my second in command as we both become partners in crime, and to work together. The Siam woman agreed happily and hugged me for the first time.

I killed the sleazy pimp on a pig farm that he owned. I cut his throat and fed the corpse to the starving pigs. The Siam woman and I celebrated by going to nightclubs, dancing all night, drinking, falling in love unconditionally, kissing and hugging each other as if we were kids again, falling in love for the first time.

Afterward, we went to a cozy Hanguk restaurant and ate the most delicious, exotic food. It was love at first sight. We talked for hours, enjoying each other's company and we both made a promise to each other. Our eyes locked, staring at each other, both of us feeling true love, heart filled with happiness and love.

I opened my eyes, seeing the reality around me for the final time and I am happy the Siam woman has kept her promise. White light filled the room and I have finally found my inner peace. I am ready to go to my new home.

The End

www.ingramcontent.com/pod-product-compliance
Lightning Source LLC
LaVergne TN
LVHW010509160826
845677LV00012B/2751

* 9 7 9 8 3 6 7 1 1 6 4 2 7 *